BROTHERS

by YIN

paintings by

CHRIS SOENTPIET

PHILOMEL BOOKS

It is warm when I finally arrive in San Francisco. I have been at sea for over a month. I can't wait to see my older brothers. I wonder if they will recognize me. It has been years since they left home. I especially miss Brother Wong as we were neither the oldest nor the youngest. I wonder if I will make new friends in America.

I stagger toward the crowd of people waiting. My knees wobble from the long voyage. Onshore, a voice calls, "Over here, Ming!"

"Hello," I say. "Are you my older brother?"

"Yes," the young man tells me in Chinese. "Do you remember me? I am Shek."

I bow to him, but I am disappointed to learn that Brother Wong has gone back to work on the dangerous railroads. I worry that I will never see him again.

"Come . . . climb up, before you fall." Shek kneels on one knee. "We are still brothers."

I can walk more steadily once we arrive in Chinatown. I whistle with amazement at my brothers' wood-framed store. Inside, the sun beams through the window where the dried sausages and ducks hang. This is proof of my brothers' hard work laying railroad tracks years earlier. Still, I am sad Brother Wong is not here.

"A year ago, there was a big fire in Chinatown," Shek tells me. "But with hard work, we opened this new store."

I look into a barrel at some rotten apples. "Do you sell these?" I ask.

"Unfortunately, most of the Chinese left Chinatown to work on the railroad up north. I am fearful there will be fewer and fewer customers coming around here." Shek sighs.

At the back of the store, Shek hoists buckets of hot water on a long wooden pole over his shoulder and pours them into a tub.

"A hot bath for a tired body," Shek says, signaling for me to get in. As I soak in my bath, Shek hands me a bowl.

I take a sip. "Yuck!"

Shek laughs. "Herbal medicine is always bitter," he says.

That evening over dried fish, duck eggs, and hot steamy noodles, Shek tells me, "We must work hard and send money home to our family in China. I found extra work farming vegetables and fruits some miles from here. I'll come back for a few days each week. Ming, you will mind the store while I am gone."

"Me?" I ask, alarmed.

I do not want to disappoint my older brother. The next morning, I get up before dawn. After breakfast of leftover porridge, Shek hands me a broom. "Sweep the front . . . stack the barrels . . . unload the baskets . . . wipe the windows. . . ." He has a long list. "And do not go past Stockton Street. Chinese should not go outside Chinatown."

I wonder why.

I watch Shek ride off to work in the darkness. It is real quiet. I have a lonely feeling.

I start my work moving heavy crates and barrels. I unravel the stitching across the top of a rice sack and use it to wipe the store clean. I help a Chinese customer load his basket with rice, tea leaves, and some white radishes. As I watch him carry his goods on the long pole, I hope for another customer.

My brother is right—only a few customers come in, and they're always Chinese. They have little money to pay for the goods and they are too few. There is nothing I can do but sit and wait.

I long for a friend.

The days pass with almost no customers.

One day, I grow curious. I look down the road and wonder what is beyond Chinatown. I dart past Stockton Street. I am met by stares and grumbles. I cannot understand the people who speak, but the look on their faces is not pleasant. I run back to the store. As I try to catch my breath, I get an idea! In my brother's closet, I find a jacket and hat. I hide my long braid under the hat and turn the brim down so no one will recognize me. I run past the road where Shek tells me not to go. I walk carefully. No one stares. My disguise is working!

I run faster as my braid falls from my big hat. Quickly I hide behind a tree. I peek and see kids playing. The sounds are unlike the silence of Chinatown. I follow the children with my eyes. Some are holding books and heading toward a big house. A school, I think. I have heard about schools in America. I would like to go. Someday.

Suddenly, I feel a tap on my shoulder. This boy with brown hair and eyes the color of the bright sky surprises me.

He points his finger to his chest and says, "PAAA-TRICK."

"Ah-PA-TOO-LICK," I mutter. I try again but have to cover my mouth and bite my cheeks to keep from laughing.

He repeats, "PAAA-TRICK."

"Ah-PA-TWO-RIC," I repeat and struggle, "PAA-TRICK." My Chinese tongue is not used to the sounds.

We both laugh.

Then I remember—I must go back to the store! I wish I knew English. But I can only wave good-bye. For now I must go back to Chinatown. I run.

The next day, I sit and wait. It is three o'clock, no customers. I think of Patrick. I want to go back! I wear my disguise and quickly run past the road and wait by that same tree. This time, a group of children swarm out of the schoolhouse. From behind, I feel a hand on my shoulder. It's Patrick!

With a sneaky grin, I push the book out of Patrick's arm and he chases me. He passes me a few times. I run after him. He runs fast, but I can run faster. We run past a busy street all the way to Chinatown. At the store, I dip my bowl into the barrel of water and offer it to my new friend.

While we rest in the store, Patrick digs in his pocket and pulls out a piece of chalk. He writes his name: P-A-T-R-I-C-K. He points to the letters and then points to himself and slowly says, "Paaaaa-trick!"

Then he points to me as if wondering what my name is. I say, "Ming!"

"Ming," he repeats. He writes the letters of my sound. I beam with delight.

I place my hand on Patrick's shoulder. I shake his hand and say, "Pun yao." This is how you say "friend" in my language.

That night, Shek comes back to town. As I help him unload the wagon, I long to go to school with Patrick. I ask, "Uhhhh, I . . . ummm . . . a school . . . I saw some kids—"

Shek interrupts in an angry voice, "I told you not to go past Stockton Street."

"But why?" I ask, my voice not so strong.

"People out there are not Chinese. Chinese are not allowed in those schools. We are safer right here in Chinatown," Shek scolds. "Just do as you are told!"

I bow my head in silence. Feeling awful for disobeying my brother, I prepare the water for his bath.

Tonight I must tell Shek about my new friend. Shek dips his hand into the water, and I say, "Ahh . . . Brother Shek, I have a new—"

"I saw you with . . . a boy," he interrupts.

I am afraid Shek will be angry. There is a long silence.

"Your new friend is nice?" he asks.

I nod. "Yes, very. He teaches me English."

Again there is a long silence. With a deep breath, he says, "Just be careful, Ming."

"I will, Older Brother. Please do not worry."

Now that Shek knows of my new friend, I look forward to seeing Patrick when he comes by the store. I don't know why he chose me as a friend. He has a caring heart. When Patrick teaches me English, I say, "More."

He shows me how to write my own name and the English alphabet—all twenty-six letters. In China, we have to remember characters to make a word. Chinese and English are very different. But every month, my English gets better and better, thanks to Patrick.

Some days he helps me at the store, and when there are no customers, we like to play marbles and toss them into the holes we dug for our game. Some days Patrick helps me clean the store.

One rainy day, Patrick invites me to his home. I am afraid of what his family will think of my almond eyes and dark long hair. My English is not so good, but with Shek's blessing, I go with Patrick to his home. He shouts, "Ming is here!"

"Ahhhhhh . . . hel-lo," I stutter. I nervously take off my hat and my long braid falls down.

From the corner of my eye, I see Mr. O'Farrell—Patrick's father—wiping his face with a wet rag. He slaps me on the back. "Hello, Ming." He pronounces my name almost right.

After checking the pot in the fireplace, Mrs. O'Farrell hugs Patrick and strokes my head. She gives us some bread. I follow Patrick's lead by dunking the bread in the soup. "You boys slow down before you choke." Her voice is soft. I do not understand everything she says, but I feel a tickle in my heart.

With his hands, Mr. O'Farrell tells me a story. In his homeland, their family had nothing to eat. So his father crossed the ocean and saved enough money to bring his family from Ireland to live in America. Mr. O'Farrell has also worked on the railroads—just like my older brothers.

After supper Mr. O'Farrell plays his flute in the air. Mrs. O'Farrell hums and claps while we boys dance out of step.

Before I leave, Mrs. O'Farrell says, "Ming, you are welcome here anytime." I smile back at her as I quickly dart down the dark gloomy road back to Chinatown.

The days Shek does not come home, I go with Patrick and have supper with his family. My English is getting better. I look forward to Mrs. O'Farrell's beef stew.

Months pass and still, only a few customers. The fruits have dried and the stalks from vegetables have turned brown with black spots. I toss out the bad ones.

One night, Shek reads a letter out loud:

"My Brothers, I may have to stay here a while longer. Since business is not good at the store, I will move east with the other railroad workers. Take care, ah-Wong."

There is a long silence. "Ming, if we don't get more customers, we will have to close the store," Shek says, clutching the letter.

I bow my head to hide my tears.

As my older brother leaves for work, Patrick asks, "What's the matter?"

"You cannot understand." My shoulders slump. "We move out. No people come to store. No pay rent."

Patrick interrupts, "But why don't you have customers? It's a great store."

I try to explain. "In Chinatown, only Chinese buy. And Chinese . . . have no money."

There is a silence. Then Patrick leans close. "Maybe you need customers who aren't Chinese. Ming, you can speak with them in English!"

We say nothing for a long time, but then Patrick's words spark a bright idea. Before he leaves, I tell Patrick my idea. I watch as a smile spreads across his face.

Early the next morning, Patrick brings a long cloth and lays it across the ground. I give him my ink and brush. He writes: GENERAL STORE—WE SPEAK ENGLISH!

Then Patrick helps me up the ladder. Thump . . . thump . . . thump . . . thump . . . thump. I nail the sign to the store. When it is finished, Patrick says, "The sign is beautiful!"

All day we wait. No one comes except an old Chinese man who stops to admire our new sign. He buys some dried mushroom ears. We wait for another customer. We kick some empty cans around and we wait. We play hide-and-seek in the store and we wait. We play some marbles and we wait.

Darkness falls. Shek should be back soon. Maybe we failed. Finally, a couple riding in a wagon points to our sign. Patrick and I jump up and guide them into the store.

"Let us help you find something," Patrick says. They walk past some almost-rotten fruits. The man buys nails by the keg. The woman buys a small bag of sugar.

I say, "Thank you," in English.

The next morning, Mr. O'Farrell and his coworkers arrive at the store. I am surprised. "Top of the morning to you!" Mr. O'Farrell shouts as he admires the lanterns. He sorts through some baskets and picks up some dried oysters. "Maybe Mrs. O'Farrell can make soup out of these!"

"Two cents," I say. Mr. O'Farrell winks at me.

Days pass, and business gets better, thanks to our new English sign. Sometimes we get four customers, sometimes ten. Today we have thirteen! Shek hauls in his wagon full of fresh greens and glowing fruits from Sacramento. He looks up at the new sign and grins. "Maybe we don't have to leave after all."

Mrs. O'Farrell tells us to stock honey, wheat, oats, and flour for our new customers. And we cannot forget the bamboo shoots, pickled vegetables, and rice for the Chinese customers, too.

Wong is back now to help at the store. We are all together.

One day, I teach Patrick Chinese. I write "hing-dai," BROTHERS. We are more than friends—we are brothers.

A FEW LAST WORDS:

The families of Patrick and Ming are fictional characters based on actual historical events. In Ireland during 1845 to 1851, over a million people starved to death or died of related diseases due to the great potato famine. Desperate for survival, many like the O'Farrells emigrated to America. The Irish hands have helped to build canal systems, coal mines, roadways, and the transcontinental railroads.

The Chinese were also important to the development and progress of early America. Before there were highways, there were mountains and dangerous terrain. Crossing from state to state was both dangerous and time-consuming. During the 1860s a plan was to have two railroad companies build railroad tracks starting at either end of the Transcontinental Railroad route. Thousands of Chinese were recruited by Central Pacific Railroad Company and built railroad tracks from Sacramento heading east. The Irish were mainly hired by the Union Pacific Railroad Company and built the railroad tracks from Nebraska heading west. The two companies would meet in the middle at Utah (refer to our book *Coolies*). The completion of the railroad track would allow passengers and cargo to cross the continent in days instead of months.

DEVELOPMENT OF CHINATOWN:

After the completion of the Transcontinental Railroad in 1869, many Chinese like Shek and Wong settled in Chinatown until cheap laborers were needed elsewhere in the United States. Once their job was completed, the Chinese were not welcomed to live anywhere else, so they returned to live in Chinatown, which was nothing more than a ghetto. In San Francisco's Chinatown, "safe" borders were set by Kearny, Stockton, Sacramento, and Pacific streets.

Early Chinese life surrounds itself with tradition, custom, and history. The Chinese were able to maintain their culture by living in Chinatown. Their survival inside Chinatown depended greatly on family and community support.

Despite the anti-Chinese sentiments, in time Chinatown flourished to become a vibrant, courageous, and proud community for the Chinese-Americans. With English signs, Chinatown became a welcoming tourist attraction. There is a Chinatown in every large city in the United States and around the world.

RESOURCES:

Cavan, Seamus. *Coming to America: The Irish-American Experience.* Brookfield, Conn.: Millbrook Press, 1993.

Daley, William. *The Immigrant Experience: The Chinese Americans.* Philadelphia: Chelsea House, 1996.

Dicker, Laverne Mau. *The Chinese in San Francisco: A Pictorial History.* New York: Dover Publications, 1979.

Feldman, Ruth Tenzer. *Don't Whistle in School: the History of America's Public Schools.* Minneapolis: Lerner Publications Company, 2001.

Genthe, Arnold, and John Kuo Wei Tchen. *Genthe's Photographs of San Francisco's Old Chinatown.* New York: Dover Publications, 1984.

Hoexter, Corinne K. *From Canton to California: The Epic of Chinese Immigration.* New York: Four Winds Press, 1976.

Hoobler, Dorothy, and Thomas Hoobler. *The Irish American Family Album.* New York: Oxford University Press, 1995.

McCunn, Ruthanne Lum. *An Illustrated History of the Chinese in America.* San Francisco: Design Enterprises of San Francisco, 1979.

Toynton, Evelyn. *Growing Up in America, 1830–1860.* Brookfield, Conn.: Millbrook Press, 1995.

"For those forgotten at the cove on the Snake River."

PATRICIA LEE GAUCH, EDITOR

PHILOMEL BOOKS   A division of Penguin Young Readers Group.   Published by The Penguin Group.   Penguin Group (USA) Inc., 375 Hudson Street, New York, NY 10014, U.S.A. Penguin Group (Canada), 90 Eglinton Avenue East, Suite 700, Toronto, Ontario, Canada M4P 2Y3 (a division of Pearson Penguin Canada Inc.).   Penguin Books Ltd, 80 Strand, London WC2R 0RL, England. Penguin Ireland, 25 St. Stephen's Green, Dublin 2, Ireland (a division of Penguin Books Ltd.).   Penguin Group (Australia), 250 Camberwell Road, Camberwell, Victoria 3124, Australia (a division of Pearson Australia Group Pty Ltd).   Penguin Books India Pvt Ltd, 11 Community Centre, Panchsheel Park, New Delhi - 110 017, India.   Penguin Group (NZ), Cnr Airborne and Rosedale Roads, Albany, Auckland 1310, New Zealand (a division of Pearson New Zealand Ltd).   Penguin Books (South Africa) (Pty) Ltd, 24 Sturdee Avenue, Rosebank, Johannesburg 2196, South Africa. Penguin Books Ltd, Registered Offices: 80 Strand, London WC2R 0RL, England.

Design by Semadar Megged.   Text set in 14-point Columbus.   The art was done in watercolors on watercolor paper.

Library of Congress Cataloging-in-Publication Data   Yin.   Brothers / by Yin ; illustrated by Chris Soentpiet.   p. cm.   Summary: Having arrived in San Francisco from China to work in his brother's store, Ming is lonely until an Irish boy befriends him.   Includes bibliographical references.   1. Chinese Americans—Juvenile fiction. [1. Chinese Americans—Fiction. 2. Friendship—Fiction. 3. Brothers—Fiction. 4. Irish Americans—Fiction. 5. San Francisco (Calif.)—History—19th century—Fiction.] I. Soentpiet, Chris K., ill. II. Title.   PZ7.Y537Bro 2006 [E]—dc22 2005032645 ISBN 0-399-23406-3   10 9 8 7 6 5 4 3 2 1 First Impression